Serena Williams

By Jon M. Fishman

AMAZING ATHLETES

Lerner Publications ◆ Minneapolis

Lerner Publications Company
A division of Lerner Publishing Group, Inc.
241 First Avenue North
Minneapolis, MN 55401 USA

For reading levels and more information, look up this title at www.lernerbooks.com.

Library of Congress Cataloging-in-Publication Data

Names: Fishman, Jon M., author.
Title: Serena Williams / by Jon M. Fishman.
Description: Minneapolis : Lerner Publications, [2017] | Series: Amazing Athletes | Includes
    bibliographical references, webography and index.
Identifiers: LCCN 2016006162 (print) | LCCN 2016007270 (ebook) | ISBN 9781512413342 (lb : alk. paper)
    | ISBN 9781512413694 (pb : alk. paper) | ISBN 9781512413700 (eb pdf)
Subjects: LCSH: Williams, Serena, 1981-—Juvenile literature. | Tennis players—United States—
    Biography—Juvenile literature. | African American women tennis players—Biography—Juvenile
    literature.
Classification: LCC GV994.W55 F57 2017 (print) | LCC GV994.W55 (ebook) | DDC 796.342092—dc23

LC record available at http://lccn.loc.gov/2016006162

Manufactured in the United States of America
1-39792-21329-3/31/2016

TABLE OF CONTENTS

Serena Williams smashes the ball during the 2015 Wimbledon championship match.

WIMBLEDON WINNER

The 2015 Wimbledon championship **match** didn't begin as expected for Serena Williams. She had already won 20 **Grand Slam** tennis titles. Her opponent, Garbine Muguruza, was playing in her first Grand Slam final. Most fans thought Serena would crush Muguruza.

Serena's **serves** were wild in the first game. Her missed shots resulted in three **double faults**. After seven games, Muguruza led the **set**, 4–3.

Serena returns a shot to Muguruza.

It was a good start for Muguruza. But Serena was the top-ranked player in the world. She would soon settle down and play with the power and skill she is known for. "[Playing against] Serena, you have to do everything perfect," said Muguruza's coach.

Serena and Muguruza *(top)* battle for the Wimbledon championship.

Serena moves to return the ball over the net.

Serena began placing her serves inside the lines on the court. She racked up **ace** after ace. When Muguruza served, Serena smashed the ball back over the net with power. Muguruza couldn't keep up. Serena won the first set, 6–4.

In the second set, Serena jumped out to a big lead, 5–1. Fans thought her victory in the match was nearly certain. But Muguruza slowly worked her way back to make the score 5–4. Serena had a chance at the **match point**. The two players smacked the ball back and forth. Then Muguruza blasted a shot over the net. The ball landed outside the line. Serena had won the match and the Wimbledon championship!

Serena smiled and put her hand over her mouth in delight. After hugging Muguruza at the net, Serena raised her arms and bounced on the court as the crowd roared. With the victory, Serena had won four Grand

Serena was 33 years old when she won Wimbledon in 2015. This made her the oldest person to win a Grand Slam tournament.

Serena holds up the trophy after winning the Wimbledon championship against Muguruza.

Slam tournaments in a row. It was the second time she had done it. Her coach, Patrick Mouratoglou, wasn't surprised by Serena's win. "She refuses defeat," Mouratoglou said. "She refuses to lose."

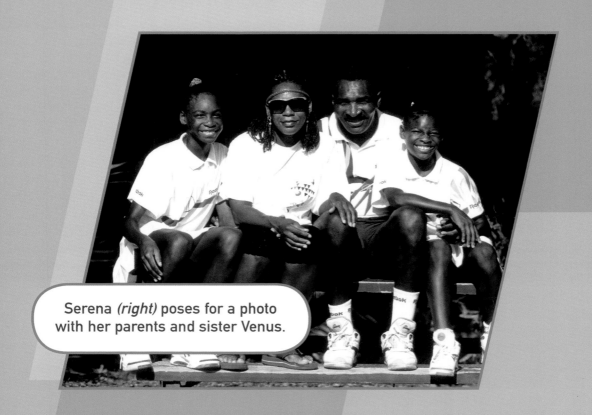

Serena *(right)* poses for a photo with her parents and sister Venus.

"FIERY SPIRIT"

On September 26, 1981, Serena Jameka Williams was born in Saginaw, Michigan. She soon moved with her family to Compton, California. Compton is in Southern California, near Los Angeles.

The warm air of Southern California makes it a great place for outdoor sports. Serena's father, Richard, began taking tennis lessons. Then he taught the sport to Serena's older sister Venus. When Serena was four years old, she began playing tennis with Richard and Venus.

Serena *(right)* and her sister Venus learned to play tennis together.

Serena is about 15 months younger than Venus. The sisters have always competed against each other. "When I'm playing her I don't think of her as my sister," Serena said.

Richard and his daughters played on tennis courts in parks all around the city. Some of the parks were dangerous places. Gang members hung around and sold drugs. Sometimes fights

Compton, shown here, could sometimes be a dangerous place to live.

broke out. But Serena and her family used the courts anyway.

It was easy to see why Serena couldn't be scared away. She loved tennis. Compton city worker Patricia Moore often saw the Williams family playing tennis when Serena was young.

Serena *(right)* and Venus both learned to play tennis from their father, Richard.

One day, Richard and Venus were practicing tough shots. "Serena was sitting on the bench, and her feet didn't even touch the court," Moore said. "Serena would yell out, 'I can do that, Dad!' She just had this fiery spirit."

Serena and Venus were talented tennis players. Richard pushed them to improve. The family practiced almost every day. The girls smashed balls to the **baseline**. They swatted

Serena *(right)* and Venus pose with former US president Ronald Reagan at a tennis camp.

balls that barely skidded over the net. They hit the ball again and again, hundreds of times a day. Richard also made sure his daughters kept up with their schoolwork. He knew a career in tennis was no sure thing.

Serena in a school yearbook photo. Serena's father encouraged her to study.

Richard taught his daughters all he knew about tennis. At nine years of age, Serena had the skills of a much older player. Venus also seemed like a tennis star in the making. Richard knew that if his daughters were to get even better, they would need a new coach.

Serena practicing tennis in Florida

GOING FOR IT

In 1991, Serena and her parents and siblings moved across the United States to West Palm Beach, Florida. Serena and Venus began working with tennis coach Rick Macci.

He picked up their lessons where Richard had left off. The sisters were **homeschooled** in Florida. This helped them spend even more time playing tennis.

Macci helped Serena become a force with a racket. Her serves sizzled through the air. She raced around the court to smash balls over the net. Her shots dazzled opponents.

The coach felt Serena could be a special tennis player. She worked hard to improve. And she always wanted to win. "Combined with the talent, that's what makes greatness," Macci said.

Venus also improved her tennis game under Macci. In 1994, she became a **professional** player. A year later, Serena followed her big sister. As professionals, Serena and Venus faced the best tennis players in the world.

The competition was fierce. But the girls slowly worked their way up the **Women's Tennis Association (WTA)** rankings.

In 1998, the sisters played against each other in a professional match for the first time. It was the second round of the Australian Open. Venus took the first two sets to win the match. "It wasn't so fun to eliminate my little sister in the second round," Venus said.

Serena *(left)* and Venus at the
1998 Australian Open

A year later, Serena and Venus played at the US Open. Venus lost to the top-ranked player in the world, Martina Hingis. But Serena won again and again. She made it all the way to the championship match against Hingis.

Serena was just the second African American woman to win the US Open. Althea Gibson won the tournament in 1957 and 1958.

The two young players battled for the US Open title. In the first set, Serena's speed and power were too much for Hingis. Serena won, 6–3. She took the lead in the second set as well. But then Hingis started to come back. The set went to a **tiebreaker**. Down by a point in the tiebreaker, Hingis hit a deep shot. Serena watched the ball sail past her and over the baseline. It was out! Serena was the US Open champion!

Serena *(right)* and Venus celebrating their gold medal win at the 2000 Summer Olympics

SERENA SLAM

Serena was playing the best tennis of her life. She competed with Venus at the 2000 Olympic Games in Sydney, Australia. The sisters teamed up and won a gold medal in **doubles**. The next year, Venus beat Serena in the final match for the US Open **singles** title. Serena wouldn't lose another Grand Slam singles match for a long time.

At the French Open in 2002, Serena had a chance for her second Grand Slam singles title. But to get it, she had to beat Venus in the final match. This time, Serena came out on top. "Hopefully, we can build a **rivalry** and we'll be able to do this a lot," Serena said.

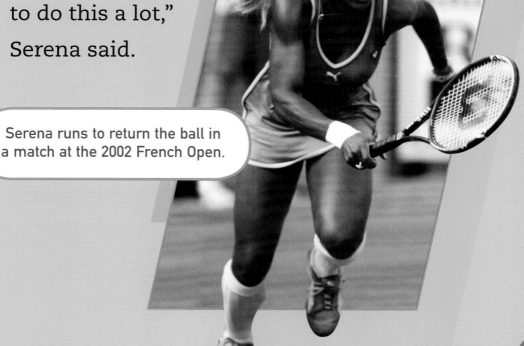

Serena runs to return the ball in a match at the 2002 French Open.

Serena went on to win Wimbledon and the US Open that year. She beat Venus in the final match of both tournaments. Serena ended 2002 ranked as the number one player in the world for the first time.

Serena has two pet dogs, and she says dogs are her favorite animal. She also likes tigers.

In 2003, the sisters battled in the championship match of the Australian Open. For the fourth time in a row, Serena beat her big sister in a Grand Slam final. The victory meant Serena was the champion of all four Grand Slam events. Fans called it the Serena Slam!

Serena had become a huge tennis superstar. She appeared on TV shows such as *The Tonight Show with Jay Leno*. Companies wanted her to help sell their products. Nike paid Serena

Serena began working with Nike to advertise their clothing and athletic gear.

millions of dollars to wear their athletic gear on the court and appear in advertisements. She even tried acting in movies and TV shows.

Serena's success was exciting. But she tried to keep her focus on tennis. A knee injury in the summer of 2003 slowed her down, and she lost her number one world ranking. She kept winning, but she wouldn't be the top-ranked player again until 2009.

Serena serves the ball in a match during the 2009 Australian Open.

MAKING HISTORY

In 2009, Serena won the Australian Open to help reclaim the top spot in the world rankings. She won Wimbledon later that year. It was her 11th Grand Slam tournament win.

Serena played great tennis over the next few years. She kept winning the biggest tournaments. In 2014, she won the US Open for the third time in a row. It marked her 18th Grand Slam win. This tied her with tennis greats Chris Evert and Martina Navratilova for the fourth most wins ever.

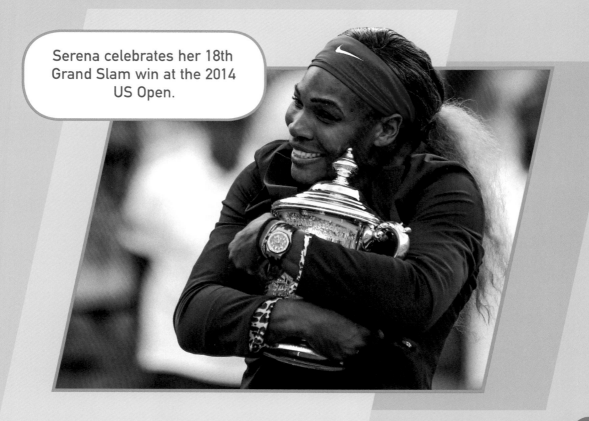

Serena celebrates her 18th Grand Slam win at the 2014 US Open.

The next year, Serena won the Australian Open and then the French Open. When she beat Garbine Muguruza to take Wimbledon, she had done it again. It was a second Serena Slam! "I've been trying to win four [Grand Slams] in a row for 12 years," she said.

The victory at Wimbledon was Serena's 21st Grand Slam singles title. Only Steffi Graf (22) and Margaret Court (24) have won more. Serena also has 15 Grand Slam doubles titles.

Serena and Venus won Olympic gold medals for doubles tennis in 2000, 2008, and 2012. In 2012, Serena also won the singles gold medal.

Serena continues to succeed off the court as well. She has been interested in fashion and design since she was a young child. With Nike, Serena helps design tennis gear that is sold around the world. She also acts when she has time between matches. In 2015, she appeared in the hit movie *Pixels*. Serena also finds time to do charity work with groups such as the Equal Justice Initiative. The group helps poor people who have been unfairly treated or wrongly sent to prison.

Serena's talent and will to win helped make her one of the most successful tennis players in the world.

Serena attends an event to promote the 2015 movie *Pixels*.

After the second Serena Slam, some fans were even calling her the best tennis player of all time. "I do want to be known as the greatest ever," she said. Serena has succeeded beyond her wildest dreams, but she isn't slowing down. She keeps pushing herself on and off the court.

Serena participates in a run to raise money for charity.

Selected Career Highlights

2015 Won Wimbledon for the sixth time to complete the second Serena Slam
Won the French Open for the third time
Won the Australian Open for the sixth time

2014 Won the US Open for the sixth time

2013 Won the US Open for the fifth time
Won the French Open for the second time

2012 Won the US Open for the fourth time
For the first time, won gold in singles at the Olympic Games
With Venus, won gold in doubles at the Olympic Games
Won Wimbledon for the fifth time

2010 Won Wimbledon for the fourth time
Won the Australian Open for the fifth time

2009 Won Wimbledon for the third time
Won the Australian Open for the fourth time

2008 Won the US Open for the third time
With Venus, won gold in doubles at the Olympic Games

2007 Won the Australian Open for the third time

2005 Won the Australian Open for the second time

2003 Won Wimbledon for the second time
Won the Australian Open for the first time to complete the first Serena Slam

2002 Ranked number one in the world for the first time
Won the US Open for the second time
Won Wimbledon for the first time
Won the French Open for the first time

2000 With Venus, won gold in doubles at the Olympic Games

1999 Won the US Open for her first Grand Slam tournament title

Glossary

ace: a serve that lands within the lines and is not touched by the receiver. An ace results in a point for the person serving.

baseline: the line at the back of a tennis court. Balls that land beyond the line are out of play.

double faults: two bad serves in a row that result in a point for the other player

doubles: a tennis match in which two-person teams play each other

Grand Slam: the name given to four tennis championships played around the world each year. The events are the Australian Open, the French Open, Wimbledon (in England), and the US Open.

homeschooled: taught at home

match: a tennis contest that is won when one player or team wins a certain number of games and sets

match point: the final point in a tennis match

professional: playing for money

rivalry: competition

serves: hits of a tennis ball to start a game

set: a group of six or more tennis games. A set must be won by at least two games or in a tiebreaker. Women's tennis matches have a maximum of three sets. A person must win two sets to win a match.

singles: a tennis match that pits one player against another

tiebreaker: a special game played to decide a winner if a set is tied 6–6

tournament: a series of contests in which a number of people or teams take part, hoping to win the championship final

Women's Tennis Association (WTA): the governing body of women's professional tennis

Further Reading & Websites

Donovan, Sandy. *Keep Your Eye on the Ball: And Other Expressions about Sports.* Minneapolis: Lerner Publications, 2013.

Gagne, Tammy. *Day by Day with Serena Williams.* Hockessin, DE: Mitchell Lane, 2016.

Savage, Jeff. *Maria Sharapova.* Minneapolis: Lerner Publications, 2014.

Serena Williams
http://serenawilliams.com
Serena's official website has all the information a fan could want about the top tennis player in the world.

Sports Illustrated Kids
http://www.sikids.com
The *Sports Illustrated Kids* website covers all sports, including tennis.

WTA
http://www.wtatennis.com
Visit the official website of the Women's Tennis Association for news about your favorite tennis players, videos, and much more.

LERNER
SOURCE

Expand learning beyond the printed book. Download free, complementary educational resources for this book from our website, www.lerneresource.com.

Index

Photo Acknowledgments

The images in this book are used with the permission of: AP Photo/ Rex Features, pp. 4, 7; AP Photo/Pavel Golovkin, pp. 5, 6; AP Photo/Kristy Wigglesworth, p. 9; © Cary Levy/Sports Illustrated/Getty Images, pp. 10, 11; © Patrick T. Fallon/Bloomberg/Getty Images, p. 12; © Paul Harris/Getty Images, p. 13; © Ken Levine/Allsport/Getty Images, p. 14; Seth Poppel Yearbook Library, p. 15; © Ken Levine/Getty Images, p. 16; © Bill Frakes/ Sports Illustrated/Getty Images, p. 18; David Bergman/KRT/Newscom, p. 20; © Francois Guillot/AFP/Getty Images, p. 21; © Kristian Dowling/Getty Images, p. 23; © Paul Crock/AFP/Getty Images, p. 24; © Bilgin S. Sasmaz/ Anadolu Agency/Getty Images, p. 25; © Julien Hekimian/WireImage/Getty Images, p. 27; Javier Galeano/Polaris/Newscom, p. 28; AP Photo/Victor R. Caivano, p. 29.

Front cover: © Cem Ozdel/Anadolu Agency/Getty Images.

Main body text set in Caecilia LT Std 55 Roman 16/28.
Typeface provided by Adobe Systems.